ANTHEM: LET GOD ARISE

Recent Researches in the Music of the Classical Era is one of four quarterly series (Middle Ages and Early Renaissance; Renaissance; Baroque Era; Classical Era) which make public the early music that is being brought to light in the course of current musicological research.

Each volume is devoted to works by a single composer or in a single genre of composition, chosen because of their potential interest to scholars and performers, and prepared for publication according to the standards that govern the making of all reliable historical editions.

Subscribers to this series, as well as patrons of subscribing institutions, are invited to apply for information about the "Copyright-Sharing Policy" of A-R Editions, Inc. under which the contents of this volume may be reproduced free of charge for performance use.

Correspondence should be addressed:

A-R Editions, Inc.
315 West Gorham Street
Madison, Wisconsin 53703

RECENT RESEARCHES IN THE MUSIC OF THE CLASSICAL ERA • VOLUME VII

Thomas Linley, Jr.

ANTHEM: LET GOD ARISE

Edited by Gwilym Beechey

A-R EDITIONS, INC. • MADISON

Contents

Preface

The Composer

The Linley family that flourished in Bath and London in the 1760s and 1770s was one of the most remarkable music families in England and Europe in the eighteenth century. Thomas and Mary Linley were the parents of twelve children, of whom at least four were leading artists and performers in their day. Thomas Linley, Jr., the third child and second son, was born at Bath on May 7, 1756. He must have shown an early aptitude for music, for he began to appear on the concert platform not only in Bath, but also in Bristol and London, at a young age. During his tragically short life, Linley was a prominent violinist, as well as one of the most promising composers on the English scene. By the time of his accidental death in a boating mishap, he had a number of large-scale works to his credit.[1]

The Music

The anthem *Let God arise* was composed in 1773 when Linley was seventeen. Written for the Three Choirs Festival at Worcester,[2] it had its first performance on the opening day of the festival, September 8, 1773, in Worcester Cathedral. Berrow's *Worcester Journal* for August 19, 1773, announced the concert as follows:

> At the Cathedral . . . a Te Deum and Jubilate, adapted to Music of the most eminent Italian composers;—a New Anthem, composed by Mr. Linley, jun. . . . and two of Mr. Handel's Coronation Anthems.
> The Principal vocal performers Miss Linley. . . . First violin by Mr. Giardini. The whole to be conducted by Mr. Isaac. The Choruses are intended to be particularly full.

The Miss Linley referred to here was the composer's younger sister Mary, who in 1773 at the age of fifteen was already much admired for her performance. Linley's older sister, Elizabeth Sheridan, sang in this festival also, and it is likely that the duet "He is a father" was sung by the two sisters.

Let God arise was performed again at the 1775 festival in Gloucester. The Linley anthem appeared on the program for the second morning of the festival (September 14, 1775) together with Handel's Dettin-gen *Te Deum*, the *Jubilate* of 1743, and one of the coronation anthems (although no sources name the anthem chosen, it was most likely the popular *Zadok*).

Linley's anthem was an exceptional achievement for a young composer of seventeen, and a work of which his teacher, William Boyce, must have been proud. The overture and the chorus "Magnify him"—a sort of double fugue in which the second fugue subject is introduced at m. 44 but is not heard completely in all parts before the first subject returns—illustrate Linley's compositional prowess. Matthew Cooke, a close associate of the Linley family in the 1770s, wrote an account of Linley's life in which he said that "this anthem confirmed his talents with the public."[3]

The text for the anthem *Let God arise* was selected from Psalm 68 as it appears in Coverdale's *Psalter*. The text is given below, together with the appropriate divisions taken from the format of the anthem:

CHORUS (Ps. 68, verse 1)

Let God arise and let his enemies be scattered:
let them that hate him flee before him.

AIR (Ps. 68, verse 3)

But let the righteous be glad and rejoice before him:

CHORUS (Ps. 68, verse 4)

O sing unto God, sing praises unto his name:

CHORUS (Ps. 68, verse 4)

Magnify him that rideth upon the heavens:
Yea and rejoice before him.

DUET (Ps. 68, verse 5)

He is a father to the fatherless and defendeth the
cause of the widow:

AIR (Ps. 68, verse 26)

Give thanks O Israel unto God in the congregation:

CHORUS (Ps. 68, verse 35)

Wonderful art thou in thy holy places, O God of
Israel: he will give strength and power unto his
people. Blessed be God. Amen.

The text underlay in the music pages of the present edition is that of the source and follows common eighteenth-century methods of capitalization and punctuation.

The Source

The only extant source of this work is contained in the Royal Music Collection of the British Museum.[4] The score was transcribed in 1780 by Joseph Gaudry and presented along with several other works by Linley to King George III. The title page of this score bears the following inscription:

ANTHEM / Composed by / Thomas Linley Jun: / Aged 17 Years. / For the Benefit of the Sons of the Clergy, / PERFORMED For the first time at the Triennial / Musical Meeting / at Gloucester / on the / 8th of September 1773.[5]

The signature of the copyist appears twice in this volume. The words "Jos. Stepn. Gaudry. Script 1780" appear on folio 53 and again on folio 75. Joseph Gaudry was an actor and singer at Drury Lane in the 1770s, who had earlier in his career been a prominent performer on the stages of the West Country.[6] Gaudry was occasionally careless and hurried, and he did not necessarily check his work. His copy of *Let God arise* was a presentation copy and, therefore, not intended for use in performance. Gaudry was evidently the professional copyist who was responsible for the production of several full scores of Linley's music that survive today in the Royal Library. Gaudry's score of *Let God arise* is the 'only extant source of the music; no autograph score or original parts have come to light, and the work has not been published.

Folios 1-53 of the source volume contain the anthem as it appears in this edition. Folios 53v-65 consist of musical settings of additional verses to the anthem. Folios 65v-75v consist of "Airs in the Song of Moses." The *Song of Moses* is an oratorio by Linley that was first performed at Drury Lane in the season of 1777 (Royal Music Collection of the British Library, R.M.21.h.9); the "Airs" are alternative settings of two of the texts set in this oratorio.

It is not known whether the additional verses to *Let God arise* were part of the original 1773 composition or were set by Linley for the second performance of the anthem at Gloucester Cathedral in 1775. No indication of where the settings of the added verses were to fit into the anthem is given in the source, and they have not been included in the present edition. The texts of the additional verses were drawn from Psalms 29 and 68; they are as follows:

RECITATIVE (Ps. 29, verses 3 and 4)

It is the Lord that commandeth the waters:
it is the glorious God that maketh the thunder.
The voice of the Lord is mighty in operation:
the voice of the Lord is a glorious voice.

AIR (Ps. 29, verses 4 and 9)

It is the Lord that ruleth the sea.
The Lord sitteth above the water-floods:
and the Lord remaineth a King for ever and ever.

AIR (Ps. 68, verses 19 and 26)

Praised be the Lord daily: even the God that
helpeth us and poureth his benefits upon us.
Give thanks O Israel unto him from the ground of
the heart.

The Edition

The edition of the anthem *Let God arise* has been prepared from Royal Manuscript 21.h.8. Obvious errors have been tacitly corrected. Editorial accidentals are enclosed in brackets; cautionary accidentals appear in parentheses. Bracketed notes such as [♩♩] and [♪♪] are given at times in the score of the present edition as a guide to the interpretation of appoggiaturas; although these interpretations are not absolute, they indicate the most natural way of performance in the context of Linley's music. Brackets enclose editorial additions and corrections made in the score. The cembalo realization is also editorial.

Performance Practice

The cembalo part as realized by the editor is a simple version that may be expanded or varied as desired by the performer. The *Basso* (continuo) part is intended for bassoon as well as for cellos, basses, and keyboard; the bassoon player should double the bass line since this seems to have been the custom in England at this period. A small group of strings and a small chorus, such as those scored for in Handel's *Chandos Anthems*, should be used to perform Linley's anthem. Two sopranos, a tenor, and a bass are required as vocal soloists.

Acknowledgments

The editor gratefully acknowledges the British Library for allowing him to use material from the manuscripts of the Royal Library now housed there.

Gwilym Beechey
University of Hull
Hull, Yorkshire, England

January 1977

Notes

1. For further biographical information on Thomas Linley, see the following: Gwilym Beechey, "Thomas Linley, junior (1756-1778)—his life, work and times" (Ph.D. diss., Cambridge University, 1965); and Gwilym Beechey, "Thomas Linley, junior (1756-1778)", *The Musical Quarterly* LIV (January 1968): 74-82.

2. See W. Shaw, *The Three Choirs Festival* (London, 1954), *passim*.

3. Matthew Cooke, *A Short Account of the late Mr. Thomas Linley, junior*, 1812, British Museum, Egerton MS 2492.

4. R.M. 21.h.8.

5. This date refers to the Worcester performance of 1773, not the Gloucester performance of 1775.

6. See A. Hare, *The Georgian Theatre in Wessex* (London, 1961), *passim*.

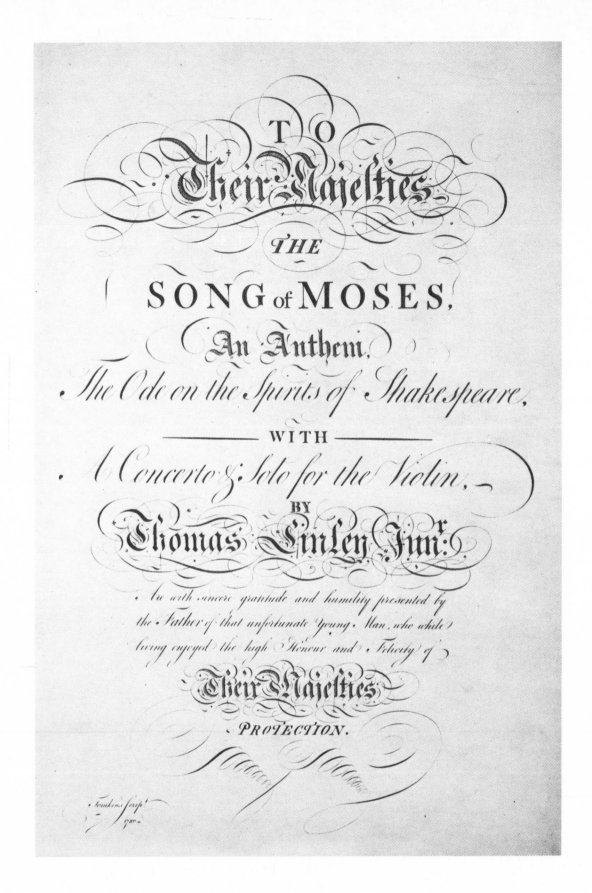

Plate I: Title page of the series of volumes containing music by Thomas Linley, Jr., and his father which Thomas Linley, Sr., presented to King George III in 1780. This title page lists the compositions included in the series of volumes. The words "An Anthem" refer to the work *Let God arise*. (Courtesy, The British Library.)

Plate II: Folio 30 of R.M. 21.h.8. written in the hand of J. S. Gaudry.
This page is taken from the chorus "Magnify Him," p. 59 of the present edition.
(Courtesy, The British Library.)

ANTHEM: LET GOD ARISE

Overture

Adagio

segue il Coro subito

Chorus: Let God arise

e-ne-mies__ be scatt- er'd, let God a- -rise and let his e- ne-mies be scatt-er'd:

e-ne-mies__ be scatt- er'd, let God a- -rise and let his e- ne-mies be scatt-er'd:

e-ne-mies be scatt- er'd, let God a- -rise and let his e-ne-mies be__ scatt-er'd:

e-ne-mies be scatt- er'd, let God a- -rise and let his e-ne-mies be scatt-

e-ne-mies be scatt- er'd, let God a- -rise and let his e-ne-mies be__ scatt-

12

14

let them that hate him, let them that hate him flee be--fore— him, let them that

let them that hate him, let them that hate him flee be--fore— him, let them that

-fore him, let them that hate— him flee be--fore him,

hate— him, let them that hate him, let them that hate him flee be--fore— him,

-fore— him, let them that hate— him flee be--fore him,

16

55

-fore him,   let them that hate him flee be--fore him, let them that hate him, let them that

- fore him,   let them that hate him flee be--fore him, let them that hate him, let them that

let them that hate him flee be--fore him, let them that hate him, let them that hate him, let them that

___ him, let them that hate him flee be--fore him,   let them that hate him, that

- fore him,   let them that hate him, let them that

scatt- er'd,   let God a - -rise_____ and let his e - ne-mies be

scatt- er'd,   let God a - -rise_____ and let his e - ne-mies be

let his e-ne-mies be scatt- er'd,   let God a - -rise   and

let his e-ne-mies be scatt- - er'd, let God a - -rise   and

let his e-ne-mies be scatt- - er'd, let God a - -rise and

God a- -rise and let his e-ne-mies be scatt-er'd,

God a- -rise and let his e-ne-mies be scatt-er'd,

let them that hate him flee be- -fore him, let them that hate him flee be-

hate him flee be- -fore him,

and let his e-ne-mies be scatt- er'd,

let them that hate him flee be- -fore him, let them that

let them that hate him flee be- -fore him, let them that

-fore him, let them that hate him flee be- -fore him, flee be-

let them that hate him flee be- -fore him, let them that hate him flee be-

let them that hate him flee be-

110

flee be- -fore him, let God a- -rise and let his e-ne-mies be

flee be- -fore him, let God a- -rise and let his e-ne-mies be

let them that hate him, let God a- -rise and let his e-ne-mies be

e-ne-mies be scatt- -er'd, let God a- -rise and let his e- ne-mies be

God a- -rise, let God a- -rise, let God a- -rise and let his e-ne-mies be

scatt-er'd: let them that hate him flee be--fore him, flee

scatt-er'd: let them that hate him flee be--fore him, flee

scatt-er'd: let them that hate him, let them that hate him, that hate him flee,

scatt-er'd: let them that hate him, let them that hate him flee,

scatt-er'd, let them that hate him flee be--fore him, let them that hate him flee be--fore him,

Air: But let the righteous

-joice _____ be-fore him, but let _____ the right-

- eous be __ glad __ and re- -joice _____

be-fore him, but let _____ the right-eous, the

But let the right - - eous be glad_ and re-joice _____

be-fore him, but let the right- - - eous be glad___ and re-

- joice _____

be-fore him, but let the right- eous, the right- eous be glad and re-

-joice _____ be--fore him, but let the right-eous, the

right- eous be glad and re--joice _____ be--fore him.

Chorus: O sing unto God

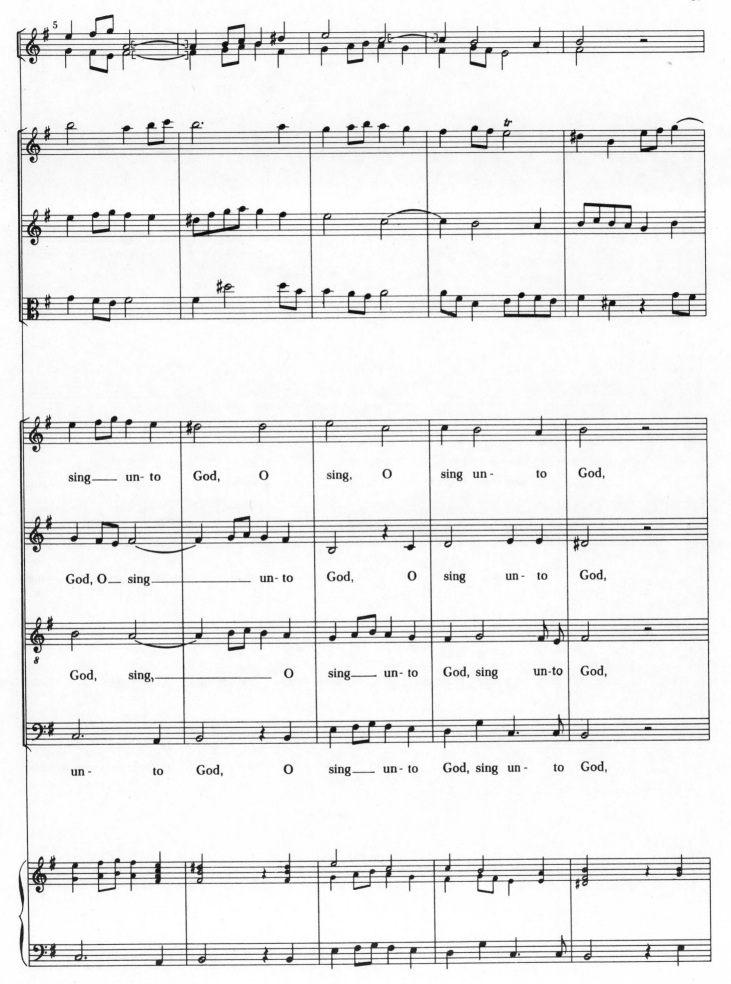

sing prai - ses un- -to _____ his name, sing

sing prai - ses un- -to his name, sing prai-ses un-to his

sing prai - ses _____ un-to his name, sing prai-ses un-to his name, sing

sing prai - ses un - to his name, sing prai-ses un-to his

prai - ses un- to his name, O sing un - to__ God, sing

sing un - to__ God, O sing, sing un - to God, sing

God, O sing un - to__ God, sing un - to God, O

God, un - to God, O sing un - to__ God, O

praises unto his name, sing prai-ses _____ un - to his name:

prai-ses un-to his name, sing prai-ses un - -to his name:

sing un - to God, sing prai-ses un - -to his name:

sing un - to God, sing prai - ses un - -to his name:

Chorus: Magnify Him

Mag-ni-fy him that ri- deth up- - on ___ the heav'ns, that ri-

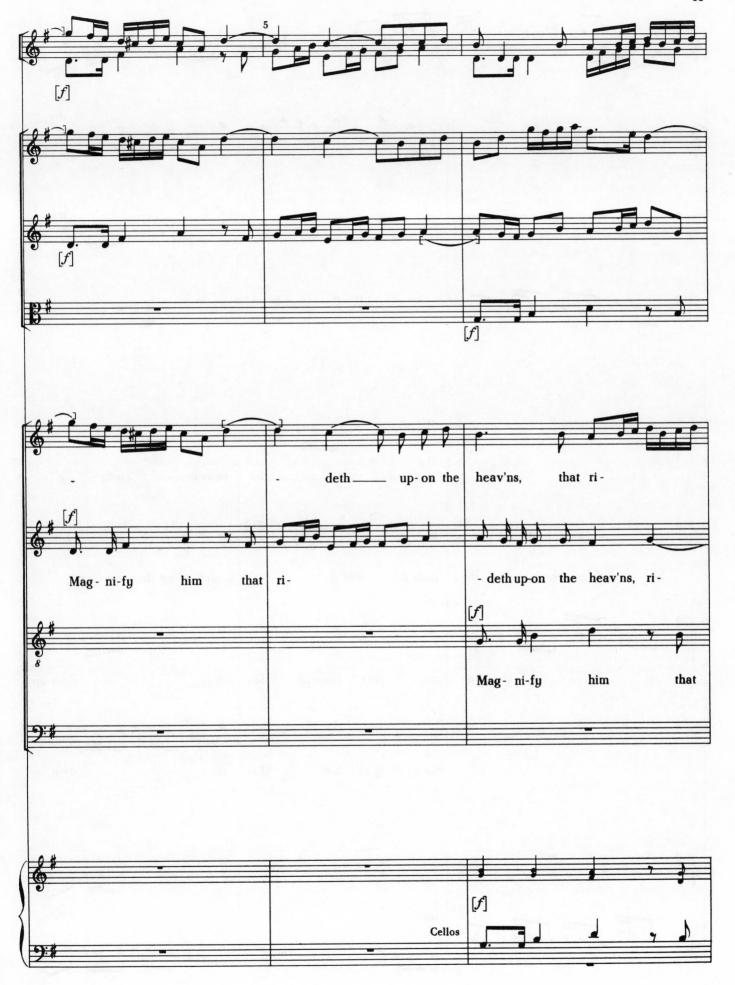

44

-fy him that ri - deth_____ up - on the heav'ns,

mag - ni - fy him that ri - deth up-on the heav'ns, that ri -

- on_____ the heav'ns, ri - - deth up-on_____ the heav'ns, mag - ni - fy

- on_____ the heav'ns, mag - ni - fy him that ri - deth up-on the heav'ns, that

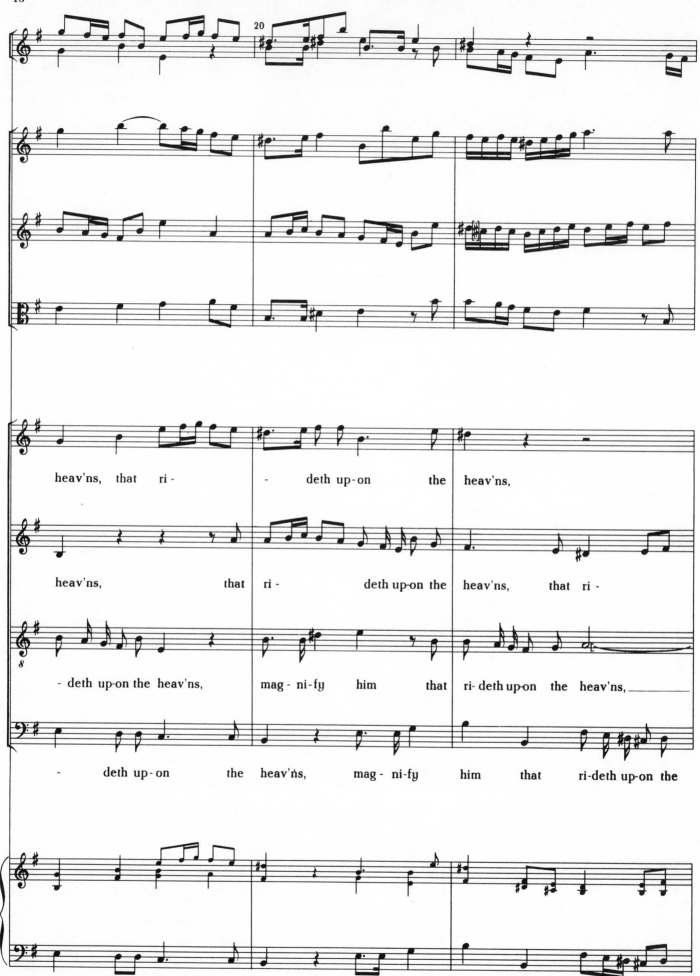

heav'ns, that ri - - deth up-on the heav'ns,

heav'ns, that ri - deth up-on the heav'ns, that ri -

- deth up-on the heav'ns, mag - ni-fy him that ri- deth up-on the heav'ns,_____

- deth up - on the heav'ns, mag - ni-fy him that ri-deth up-on the

52

ri-deth up-on the heav'ns, mag- - ni-fy him that ri-deth up-on the heav'ns.

- ni- fy him that ri-deth up-on the heav'ns, that ri-deth up-on the heav'ns.

ri-deth up-on the heav'ns, that ri-deth up-on the heav'ns, that ri-deth up-on the heav'ns.

ri-deth up-on the heav'ns, that ri-deth up-on the heav'ns, that ri-deth up-on the heav'ns.

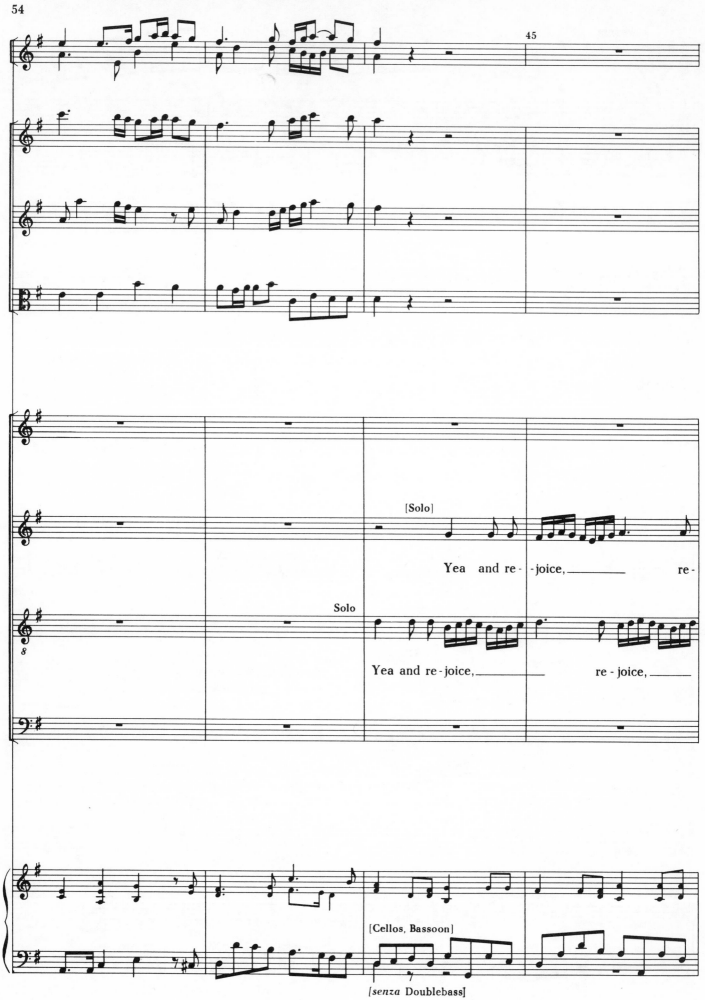

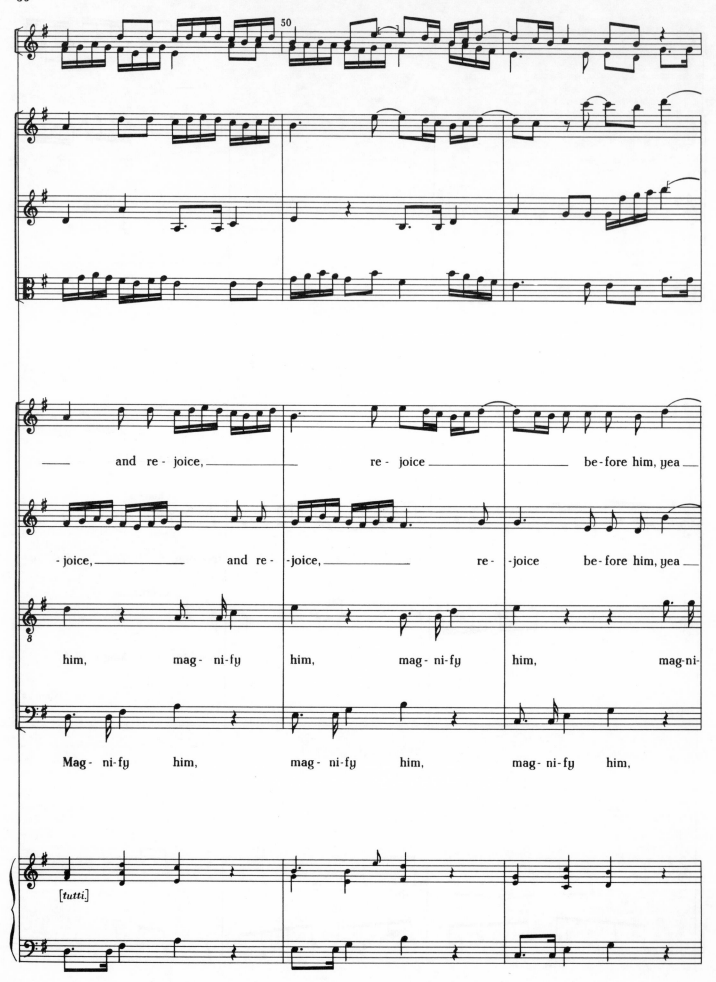

and re-joice,_____ re-joice_____ be-fore him, yea

-joice,_____ and re--joice,_____ re--joice be-fore him, yea

him, mag-ni-fy him, mag-ni-fy him, mag-ni-

Mag-ni-fy him, mag-ni-fy him, mag-ni-fy him,

[tutti.]

magni-fy him, magni-fy him, yea and re-joice_____

him, mag - ni-fy him, mag - ni-fy him, yea and re -

-fore him, yea and re-joice_____ be-fore him, mag-ni-fy

yea and re-joice_____ be-fore him, mag-ni-fy him,

61

Duet: He is a father

(a) Because all the beamed groups of three eighth-notes in this duet are triplets, the editor considers the addition of "3's" throughout the piece unnecessary. The rhythms ♪♪♪ and ♪.♪ always fit together, and the sixteenth-note should always be played with the third note of the triplet.

64

cause__ of the wi - dow.

cause__ of the wi - dow.

Air: Give thanks O Israel

thanks, give thanks, O Is- rael, un- to__ God in the con- - ga- tion, in the

con- - ga- tion, give thanks, give thanks, O Is- rael, un- to__ God, O

Is- rael, un- to God__ in the con- gre- ga- tion.

Give thanks, give thanks, O Is- rael,_un- to_ God, give

thanks, give thanks, O__ Is- rael,_un- to God in the con- -ga-tion, in the

con- -gre- -ga- tion, give thanks,_____ O Is- rael,_un-to God in the

con- -gre- -ga-tion, give thanks, give thanks, O Is- rael, un-to

God, O Is- rael,_un-to_ God, give thanks,_ give thanks, O Is- rael,_un-to

God, give thanks, give thanks, O Is - rael, un - to__ God. O Is - rael, un - to

God__ in the con - gre - ga - tion.

segue subito il Coro

Chorus: Wonderful art thou

strength _____ and pow'r un-to his peo - ple, he will give strength_____ and___

pow'r_____ un-to his peo - ple, he will give strength, he will give strength and pow'r

will give strength_____ and pow'r un-to his peo - ple, he will give

strength and pow'r___ un-to his peo - ple, he will give strength, he will give strength _____

un- to his peo- ple, he will give strength and pow'r un- to his

strength un- to his peo- ple, he will give strength and pow'r un- to his

un- to his peo- ple, he will give strength and pow'r un- to his

pow'r un- to his peo- ple, he will give strength and pow'r un- to his

peo- ple.

peo- ple.

peo- ple.

peo- ple.

Bless- -ed be God. A- -men, A- -men, A- - men, A-

Bless- -ed be God. A- -men, A- -men, A- - men, A-

Bless- -ed be God. A- -men, A- -men, A- - men, A-

Bless- -ed be God. A- -men, A- -men, A- - men, A-

-men. He will give strength and pow'r un- to his peo-ple, he will give

-men. He will give strength and pow'r un- to his peo-ple, he will give

-men. He will give strength and pow'r un- to his peo-ple, he will give

-men. He will give strength and pow'r un- to his peo-ple, he will give

strength and pow'r un-to his peo-ple, he will give strength un-to his

strength and pow'r un-to his peo-ple, he will give strength and pow'r un-to his

strength and pow'r, he will give strength and

strength and pow'r un-to his peo-ple, he will give strength, will give strength and

strength _____ ___ and pow'r, give strength and pow'r,

peo- ple. Bless- -ed be God, he will give

peo- ple, he___ will give strength and pow'r, give strength and

___ he will give strength and pow'r un-to___ his peo- ple.

he will give strength____ and_ pow'r un- -to____ his peo-ple.

strength,___ give strength____ and_ pow'r. A- -men, A- -men, he will give

pow'r, he will give strength and pow'r. Bless- -ed be God, he will give

Bless- -ed be God. A- -men, A- -men, A-

strength _____ and pow'r_____ un - to his peo-ple. A - -men, A -

he will give strength and pow'r un-to his peo-ple. A - -men, A -

strength _____ and pow'r un- -to his peo-ple. A - -men, A -

-men, he will give strength and pow'r un-to his peo-ple. A - -men, A -

Adagio

pow'r un-to__ his__ peo-ple. Bless- -ed be God. A- -men, A- -men.

pow'r_____ un-to his peo-ple. Bless- -ed be God. A- -men, A- -men.

pow'r un- to his peo-ple. Bless- -ed be God. A- -men, A- -men.

pow'r un- to his peo-ple. Bless- -ed be God. A- -men, A- -men.